W9-CRY-333

Ryan Howard

By Jeff Savage

AMAZING ATHLETES

Lerner Publications Company • Minneapolis

Copyright © 2008 by Jeff Savage

All rights reserved. International copyright secured. No part of this book may be reproduced, stored in a retrieval system, or transmitted in any form or by any means—electronic, mechanical, photocopying, recording, or otherwise—without the prior written permission of Lerner Publishing Group, Inc., except for the inclusion of brief quotations in an acknowledged review.

Lerner Publications Company
A division of Lerner Publishing Group, Inc.
241 First Avenue North
Minneapolis, MN 55401 U.S.A.

Website address: www.lernerbooks.com

Library of Congress Cataloging-in-Publication Data

Savage, Jeff, 1961–
    Ryan Howard / by Jeff Savage.
        p.   cm. — (Amazing athletes)
    Includes index.
    ISBN 978-0-8225-8833-7 (lib. bdg. : alk. paper)
    1. Howard, Ryan James, 1979– —Juvenile literature. 2. Baseball players—United States—Biography—Juvenile literature. 3. Philadelphia Phillies (Baseball team)—Juvenile literature. I. Title.
GV865.H67S38 2008
796.357092—dc22 [B]   2007025133

Manufactured in the United States of America
1 2 3 4 5 6 – DP – 13 12 11 10 09 08

TABLE OF CONTENTS

Ryan Howard gets a hit during the Philadelphia Phillies game against the Washington Nationals on September 30, 2007.

FIGHTIN' PHILLIES

The bases were loaded for Ryan Howard. The Philadelphia Phillies first baseman stood tall in the **batter's box**. He stared at the pitcher and gripped his bat with both hands.

The game was in the third inning. The Phillies were leading the Washington Nationals, 1–0. But they wanted to score more runs. Ryan and his teammates needed one more win to make the **playoffs**.

The pressure was on. But Ryan was not nervous. He loves these moments. He loves being the guy everyone is counting on. Ryan is his team's most powerful hitter. In fact, he might be the most powerful hitter in baseball.

Washington pitcher Jason Bergmann threw a pitch toward the plate. Ryan swung hard. Crack! The ball sailed into right field for a base hit! Carlos Ruiz and Jimmy Rollins crossed home plate. Ryan had helped give his team a 3–0 lead.

The Phillies could relax a little, but not too much. Ryan's team was playing its final game of the 2007 **regular season**. The Phillies were tied with the New York Mets for first place in the **National League (NL)** East **standings**. Just a few weeks ago, the Phillies had been seven games behind the Mets. No one believed the Phillies could catch New York. But Ryan's team kept battling. They had made an unbelievable comeback.

By the seventh inning, the Phillies had a

5–1 lead. Ryan came to the plate once more. The fans at Citizens Bank Park in Philadelphia stood cheering. Nationals pitcher Mike Bacsik threw a **fastball** toward the plate. Ryan swung and smashed the ball high into the sky. It rocketed over the wall and landed in the upper deck for a monster **home run**. The Phillies won the game, 6–1.

"Unbelievable!" Ryan shouted as he celebrated with his teammates. "A lot of people counted us out," he said. "But . . . we just stayed with it. That's why they call us the Fightin' Phillies."

Ryan celebrates in front of fans after the Phillies won the game against the Nationals to go to the playoffs.

Ryan was born in Saint Louis, Missouri, home of the famous Gateway Arch.

A Playful Boy

Ryan James Howard was born November 19, 1979, in Saint Louis, Missouri. Ryan's parents, Ron and Cheryl, taught their children to be confident. They told their kids to never use the word "can't." Ryan's twin brother, Corey; older brother, Chris; and sister, Roni, all did well in school.

Ryan was a big, playful boy. He liked to tell jokes and had lots of friends at school. But he was serious when it was time for schoolwork. His favorite subject was history.

Ryan's favorite sport was baseball. As a big, strong left-hander, first base was a natural position for him. His nickname was Hurt because he hit the ball so hard. "When he made contact, it was like, 'Wow!'" said his brother Corey. "His home runs were loud."

By the age of 12, Ryan had become a monster batter at the plate. In one Little League game, he bashed a ball way over the fence. It sailed so far that it landed on the roof of a restaurant 430 feet away. "That ball was flying," said his mother, Cheryl. "That was one of the first times I thought he could be a major leaguer one day."

Ryan played football on this field at Lafayette High School in Missouri.

Ryan enjoyed a fun, busy life at Lafayette High School. In the fall, he played on the football team. He also played the trombone in the marching band. Practicing both was not easy. Most days, Ryan ran straight from the football field to band practice nearby. "He would throw

Ryan has several nicknames. Here are some of them: "Powered Howard" "Rhino" "Man-Mountain" "One-Man Gang."

his shoulder pads to the side and play the trombone in his cleats," said Phil Milligan, the school's band director.

In the winter, Ryan played on the basketball team. He gobbled up rebounds and blocked shots. In the spring came his favorite sport—baseball. He set a school record with 17 career home runs. His powerful swings became legendary. Once he bashed a ball so hard that it ripped the glove off an outfielder's hand.

Ryan looked as if he had the hitting skills to be a pro baseball player. But another part of Ryan's game needed to get better.

Ryan always tries to do his best. "I try to be as close to perfect as I can," he says. "You can never reach perfection, but you can still strive for it."

Ryan catches a foul ball in 2004. As a young player, Ryan had to work hard on his fielding.

HARD AT WORK

Throughout high school, Ryan struggled with his fielding. This might be the reason why major-league **scouts** chose not to **draft** him for their teams. Colleges weren't interested in him, either.

Ryan's high school coach, Steve Miller, couldn't believe it. He called coach Keith Guttin at nearby Southwest Missouri State University. "Someone is missing the boat with this kid," Miller said. Guttin decided to give Ryan a chance.

Coach Guttin's decision paid off. Ryan went on to become one of the school's all-time best players. In three college seasons, he smashed 50 home runs!

After his third year, the Phillies selected him in the fifth round of the 2001 draft.

The Phillies drafted Ryan after his third year of college. Ryan did not earn his degree—yet. Ryan plans to return to college to finish what he started. "It's a requirement and an expectation. He understands that," says his father, Ron. Ryan will take college classes when he can. And he wants to graduate. "Yep, I know it's something I'm going to have to do. And I will," he says.

Like most players, Ryan began his pro career in the **minor leagues**. He would have to learn and improve. If he was good enough and worked hard enough, he would earn his way to the **major leagues**.

Ryan did just that. And he did it in less than three seasons. He smashed the ball out of minor-league stadiums around the country.

Ryan played first base in the minor leagues.

By late 2004, he was leading the minor leagues with 46 home runs and 131 **runs batted in (RBIs)**. On September 1, the Phillies called him up to the big-league team. Ryan's lifelong dream had come true. He was a Major League Baseball player.

In his first game for the Phillies, he struck out. But soon he got his first major-league hit. Two days later he got his first double. Three days after that he blasted his first big-league home run in an 11–9 win against the New York Mets.

Ryan's career was starting out well. The Phillies and their fans were excited about their talented young first baseman. But there was one problem. The Phillies already had a star first baseman—Jim Thome. Where was Ryan going to play?

Ryan improved his game in the minor leagues. He had to work hard to win a place on the Phillies team.

TAKING OVER

As the 2005 season began, the Phillies weren't sure what to do. In **spring training**, they tried playing Ryan in the outfield. He struggled with fielding. So the team sent him down to the minors.

Ryan was frustrated, but he stayed positive. "We taught Ryan earlier in life that if you keep working hard, eventually you'll get the prize you are seeking," said his father.

One month into the season, Thome hurt his elbow. The Phillies called up Ryan to play first base. In his first game, he smacked three hits in a 4–3 win over the Cincinnati Reds.

Jim Thome plays first base for the Phillies in a game in June 2005.

As the weeks passed, Ryan got some big hits. But he also struck out too much. At one point in the season, his **batting average** was just .218. "He was trying too hard, over-swinging, and trying to show how good he is," said Phillies manager Charlie Manuel.

Meanwhile, Jim Thome got healthy. When Thome was ready to play, the Phillies sent Ryan back to the minors. No one would have blamed Ryan for being upset. But he did not complain or sulk. Instead, he pounded the ball. He was soon leading his

Ryan has a great attitude. He is gentle and focused. He never seems to get mad. "The only thing that sets him off is hearing people say he can't do things," says his brother Corey. "They've said he can't hit lefties, he can't hit for a high average. Whatever they've said Ryan can't do, he's gone out and done."

league in batting average. His upbeat attitude was paying off.

At the end of June, Thome got hurt again. Ryan was called up on July 1. "We'll bring him up and see what he can do," said Manuel.

In Ryan's second game, he blasted a three-run homer against the Braves. Soon after, he crushed a game-winning homer to beat the Los Angeles Dodgers. Then he beat the Braves and Dodgers again with game-winning **grand slams**! "He was completely different when he came back up. More relaxed," said Manuel.

Phillies manager Charlie Manuel watches a 2005 game from the dugout.

Ryan was having fun now. The **rookie** greeted teammates each day with a dozen handshakes. "There's a lot of [strength] in those hands," said teammate Jimmy Rollins.

With Thome out for the rest of the season,

Ryan powered the Phillies on an exciting playoff chase. He blasted 22 home runs in just 88 games!

Ryan bats in a 2005 game against the San Diego Padres.

Ryan celebrates after hitting a home run in a September 2005 game.

But the Phillies missed making the playoffs by a single game. "It was a fun run," said Ryan. "We showed a lot of heart, a lot of fight."

After the season, Ryan was named National League (NL) Rookie of the Year. "He honestly carried the team," said pitcher Billy Wagner. "I've never seen a kid have such an impact that soon, just come up and really take over a team."

Ryan became the Phillies starting first baseman in 2006.

PHAN FAVORITE

Before the start of the 2006 season, the Phillies announced a trade. They sent Thome to the Chicago White Sox for several players. First base belonged to Ryan. He was ready for a huge season.

Ryan didn't just hit home runs in 2006. He hit massive home runs! In one game, he crushed the ball 496 feet into the stands. It was the longest home run ever hit at Philadelphia's Citizens Bank Park. In another game, he bashed a homer into the third deck, 481 feet away. By midseason, he was leading the majors with 30 home runs. Ryan was a Phillies "Phan Favorite." His huge fan club called itself Howard's Homers.

Ryan signs autographs for fans. He became a Phillies "Phan Favorite" during the 2006 season.

Ryan was popular nationwide too. Fans voted him onto the National League team for the 2006 Major League **All-Star Game** at PNC Park in Pittsburgh. The day before the game, he competed against baseball's best sluggers in the **Home Run Derby**. Ryan hit 23 home runs. He even whacked several balls out of the stadium and into the nearby Allegheny River. Ryan won the derby.

Ryan hits a home run in the final round of the Home Run Derby at the All-Star Game in 2006.

By this time, Ryan had become a hero in Philadelphia. Fans asked him for his autograph wherever he went. Women held up signs at the ballpark asking him to marry them. One fan even ran onto the field and bowed to him in the batter's box!

The excitement continued. In late August, Ryan homered in four straight games. His 48th home run tied the Phillies' record for most in a season. Two days later, Ryan drilled one into the upper deck at RFK Stadium against the Nationals to break the team record. The mark belonged to one of the all-time greatest Phillies players—Mike Schmidt. The legendary third baseman was impressed with Ryan. "He might be more dangerous than Barry Bonds ever was in his prime," Schmidt said.

Ryan didn't stop there. Four days later, he crushed three homers in an 8–7 win over the Braves. He finished the season with a major-league-best 58 home runs. This was a record for a second-year player.

Ryan also led the majors in RBIs with 149. His incredible stats earned him the 2006 National League **Most Valuable Player (MVP) Award**. He beat out another superstar first baseman—Albert Pujols of the St. Louis Cardinals.

Ryan poses with the 2006 National League MVP Award.

The Phillies are a much better team when Ryan is playing well.

Phillies fans expected great things from Ryan in 2007. But a leg injury slowed him down early in the season. Without their best hitter, the team struggled to win games.

But as Ryan started playing better, so did the Phillies. They got on a roll in the season's final month. They passed the Mets on the final day to match the biggest comeback in major-league history. As usual, Ryan led the way with 47 homers and 136 RBIs.

The Phillies' playoff hopes ended quickly, though. The Colorado Rockies swept them in three straight games. At first, Ryan was disappointed. Still, he realized that his team had made a big step forward. "The experience didn't turn out the way we wanted," he said. "But now we know what [making the playoffs] feels like. We'll go into next year and want to go further."

With Ryan in the lineup, the Phillies are sure to go far. And his powerful hitting will give fans plenty to cheer about. "I just want to play as hard as I can, be the best I can, and be remembered for that," says Ryan.

Selected Career Highlights

2007   Finished second in the National League in home runs, with 47
Finished second in the National League in runs batted in, with 136
Reached 100 career home runs faster than any other major-
league player, hitting his 100th in just 325 games
Earned his first career stolen base against the Los Angeles
Dodgers

2006   Won NL Most Valuable Player Award
Led Major League Baseball in home runs with 58
Led MLB in runs batted in with 149
Became first Phillies player to hit more than 50 home runs in a
season
Named NL Player of the Month for August
Named NL Player of the Month for September
Won Home Run Derby at the All-Star Game

2005   Named NL Rookie of the Year
Led MLB rookies with 22 home runs
Broke MLB rookie record for home runs in September with 10

2004   Played in first major-league game for Philadelphia Phillies on
September 1
Led minor leagues with 46 home runs and 131 runs batted in
Named MVP of the Eastern League (minor league) as member of
Reading (Pennsylvania) Phillies

2003   Named MVP of the Florida State League (minor
league) as a member of the Clearwater Threshers
Led the Florida State league with a .304 batting
average
Led the Florida State league in home runs
with 23

2002   Led all Phillies minor leaguers in home
runs with 19, while playing for the
Lakewood Blue Claws (New Jersey)
Named to South Atlantic League All-Star
team

2001   Selected in the fifth round of the MLB
draft
Finished college career with 50 home runs

Glossary

All-Star Game: a special game held in July each year between a group of the best major league players, as voted by fans

batter's box: the rectangular area on each side of home plate in which the batter stands

batting average: a statistic that shows a player's success at hitting the ball. For example, if a hitter gets 3 hits in 10 at-bats, the batting average would be .300.

draft: to choose a player for a pro team. Also a yearly event in which professional teams take turns choosing new players from a selected group.

fastball: a fast pitch that usually travels straight

grand slams: home runs in which there are runners on all the bases. These home runs produce four runs.

home run: a hit that allows a batter to circle all the bases in one play to score a run

Home Run Derby: a contest held every year the night before the All-Star Game. In this contest, a selected group of players compete to see who can hit the most home runs.

major leagues: the top level of professional baseball. Major League Baseball (MLB) is divided into the National League and the American League.

minor leagues: a group of teams where players work to improve their skills and prepare to move to the major leagues

Most Valuable Player (MVP) Award: an award given each year to the player who has been judged to have been the most valuable player to his team that season

National League (NL): one of baseball's two major leagues. The National League includes the Philadelphia Phillies, Atlanta Braves, New York Mets, Cincinnati Reds, and others.

playoffs: games played to decide which team is the Major League Baseball champion

regular season: the 162-game schedule that each major-league team plays to decide who will make the playoffs

rookie: a player who is in his or her first season

runs batted in (RBIs): the number of runners able to score on a batter's action, such as a hit or a walk

scouts: people who judge the skills of players. Scouts work for individual teams and help them decide whom to draft.

spring training: a time from February through March when baseball teams train for the season

standings: a listing of the teams in a league or division in order of their number of wins and losses

Further Reading & Websites

Kelly, James. *Baseball*. New York: DK Publishing, 2005.

Savage, Jeff. *Albert Pujols*. Minneapolis: Lerner Publications Company, 2007.

Savage, Jeff. *Barry Bonds*. Minneapolis: Lerner Publications Company, 2008.

The Official Site of Major League Baseball
http://www.mlb.com
Major League Baseball's official website provides fans with the latest scores and game schedules, as well as information on players, teams, and baseball history.

Philadelphia Phillies: The Official Site
http://philadelphiaphillies.com
The official website of the Philadelphia Phillies includes the team schedule and game results, late-breaking news, biographies of Ryan Howard and other players and coaches, and much more.

Sports Illustrated for Kids
http://www.sikids.com
The *Sports Illustrated for Kids* website covers all sports, including baseball.

Index

Photo Acknowledgments

The images in this book are used with the permission of: © Chris
Gardener/Getty Images, pp. 4, 7; © Panoramic Images/Getty Images,
p. 8; © Kimberly Kraichely, p. 10; AP Photo/Susan L. Angstadt, p. 12;
© SWB Yankees, pp. 14, 16; © Rich Pilling/MLB Photos/Getty Images,
p. 17; © George Gojkovich/Getty Images, p. 18; © Rob Leiter/MLB Photos/
Getty Images, p. 20; © Jamie Squire/Getty Images, p. 21; AP Photo/Rusty
Kennedy, p. 22; AP Photo/Kathy Willens, p. 23; AP Photo/Bill Kostroun,
p. 24; AP Photo/Charles Krupa, p. 26; © Mitchell Layton/Getty Images,
p. 27; © Jim McIsaac/Getty Images, p. 29.

Front cover: AP Photo/George Widman.